Pinocchio

Illustrated by Pam Storey.

© 1994 Grandreams Limited. This edition
Published by
Grandreams Limited
Jadwin House, 205/211 Kentish Town Road, L

Printed in Italy.

D0962546

One day a carpenter picked up a log of wood from a pile in the corner of his workshop. He was just about to chop it with his axe when he heard a little voice cry, "Don't hurt me!" The voice came from the log of wood.

The carpenter was so terrified that he opened the door and was about to throw the log away, when who should come by, but Geppetto the toy maker. "Just what I need," cried the old man. "I am going to carve a puppet that will behave just like a real boy."

The carpenter was pleased to get rid of the talking log, because he thought it was bewitched!

Back at his toy shop Geppetto started work straight away. First he carved the puppet's head, and an amazing thing happened...the eyes blinked and the mouth smiled. Next he carved the body right down to the toes.

All of a sudden the puppet's foot
flew up and kicked the old man on the
nose. Instead of being angry, Geppetto was delighted with
his talking puppet. "I shall call you Pinocchio," he smiled,
"and you shall call me Father."

Geppetto began to teach Pinocchio how to walk. No sooner had the puppet learned, than he dashed out of the door and ran off down the street. Suddenly, a large policeman stepped out in front of Pinocchio and grabbed him.

By now a crowd had gathered and Geppetto was shouting at Pinocchio for running away. The angry crowd told the policeman to lock the old man up, for he was being cruel to the puppet.

So the policeman took poor Geppetto away to prison and Pinocchio ran off home.

You will have guessed by now that Pinocchio had a mind of his own, and was going to do exactly as he pleased!

Later on, Geppetto was let out of prison because he had done nothing wrong. He made Pinocchio promise that he would go to school and learn to read.

That night, Geppetto made him some new clothes.
"All I need now Father, is a spelling book," said
Pinocchio. "Then I shall be like other boys."

At once, the kind old man went out into the cold
night and sold his only coat to buy the spelling book.

Next morning, Pinocchio set off to school. But what was that wonderful sound he could hear? It was the music of a fairground.

He forgot all about school when he spotted a 'Puppet Theatre'. Without a second thought Pinocchio sold his spelling book to buy a ticket to go inside.

But when the puppets saw Pinocchio, they shouted for him to come up on stage to join them. The whole performance was ruined! The puppeteer threatened to throw Pinocchio on the fire, like a log of wood.

However, Pinocchio cried so pitifully that the puppeteer gave him five pieces of gold to take to Geppetto.

On his way home, Pinocchio met a sly fox and a cat who pretended to be blind. They told the puppet that if he buried his gold in a certain field, a miracle would happen - a tree would grow, laden with gold pieces.

It was a trick of course! And when Pinocchio returned the next day, the five gold pieces had gone and so had the fox and the cat.

Not content with stealing Pinocchio's money, the fox and cat disguised themselves as robbers and grabbed Pinocchio. They hung him from a tree and then ran off.

Luckily for Pinocchio, the Blue Fairy lived nearby and she saved him. She sent her poodle dog footman to fetch the doctors...and what strange doctors they turned out to be...a crow, an owl and a cricket.

They all decided that Pinocchio was not dead after all, he was just a wicked puppet that had run away.

The Blue Fairy asked Pinocchio to tell her about his adventures, but the puppet would not tell the truth. The more he lied, the longer his nose grew. It grew so long it stuck out of the window.

The Blue Fairy clapped her hands and several birds flew down. They pecked at Pinocchio's nose until it was the right size once more.

"That's what comes of telling lies!" laughed the Blue Fairy.

"How can I become a real boy?" Pinocchio asked the Blue Fairy.

"If you are good and go to school, you will have your dearest wish," she promised.

So Pinocchio went back to school. He worked hard, but unfortunately he soon grew tired of being good. He made friends with the naughtiest boy in the class.

One night they decided to run away to Toyland (where there is no school). They climbed into a special coach pulled by donkeys, and off they went.

It seemed fun at first, no lessons or work for months. Pinocchio and his friend loved it.

Then, without warning, Pinocchio woke up one day to find he had grown a pair of donkey's ears. His friend had already changed into a donkey. All the children who came to Toyland were changed into donkeys and then sold.

A circus ringmaster bought poor Pinocchio and worked him very hard. One day, when he was jumping through a hoop, he hurt his leg.

The circus didn't want a lame donkey, so Pinocchio was sold again, this time to a man who wanted to make the donkey's skin into a drum.

He dragged Pinocchio into the sea to drown him, but the puppet slipped out of the skin and swam away laughing.

Suddenly a great whale rose up from the waves. Its monstrous jaws opened up wide and swallowed Pinocchio in one gulp.

Down and down went the puppet right to the bottom of the whale's stomach. He felt very frightened, until he heard a voice he knew.

There was old Geppetto sitting in a boat, carving toys from the fish bones lying around.

Geppetto explained that he had gone to sea to look for Pinocchio and had been swallowed by the whale. He had lived on the food he had packed in his boat.

With the help of the Blue Fairy, the two sailed out of the whale's mouth and arrived safely back home.

Pinocchio sat down with Geppetto and told him all about his adventures. He promised never to leave the old man again.